# Peter Pan

Régis Loisel

## Book One
## London

To James Matthew Barrie.
To the wonderful Disney team,
which turned Barrie's Peter Pan
into the marvel we all know.
A big thank you to everyone.
They won't contradict me:
Peter Pan exists.
Here's the proof...

—Régis Loisel

# Peter Pan

book one London

written and illustrated
by Régis Loisel
translated by Mary Irwin
edited by Greg S. Baisden
lettered by Roxanne Starr

originally published in 1990 by Éditions Vent d'Ouest, Issy Les Moulineaux
North American Edition

320 Riverside Dr., Northampton MA 01060


ISBN 1-879450-42-9

Printed in France

# Peter Pan

*written and illustrated by*

Régis
Loisel

Freely based on the characters of Sir James Matthew Barrie

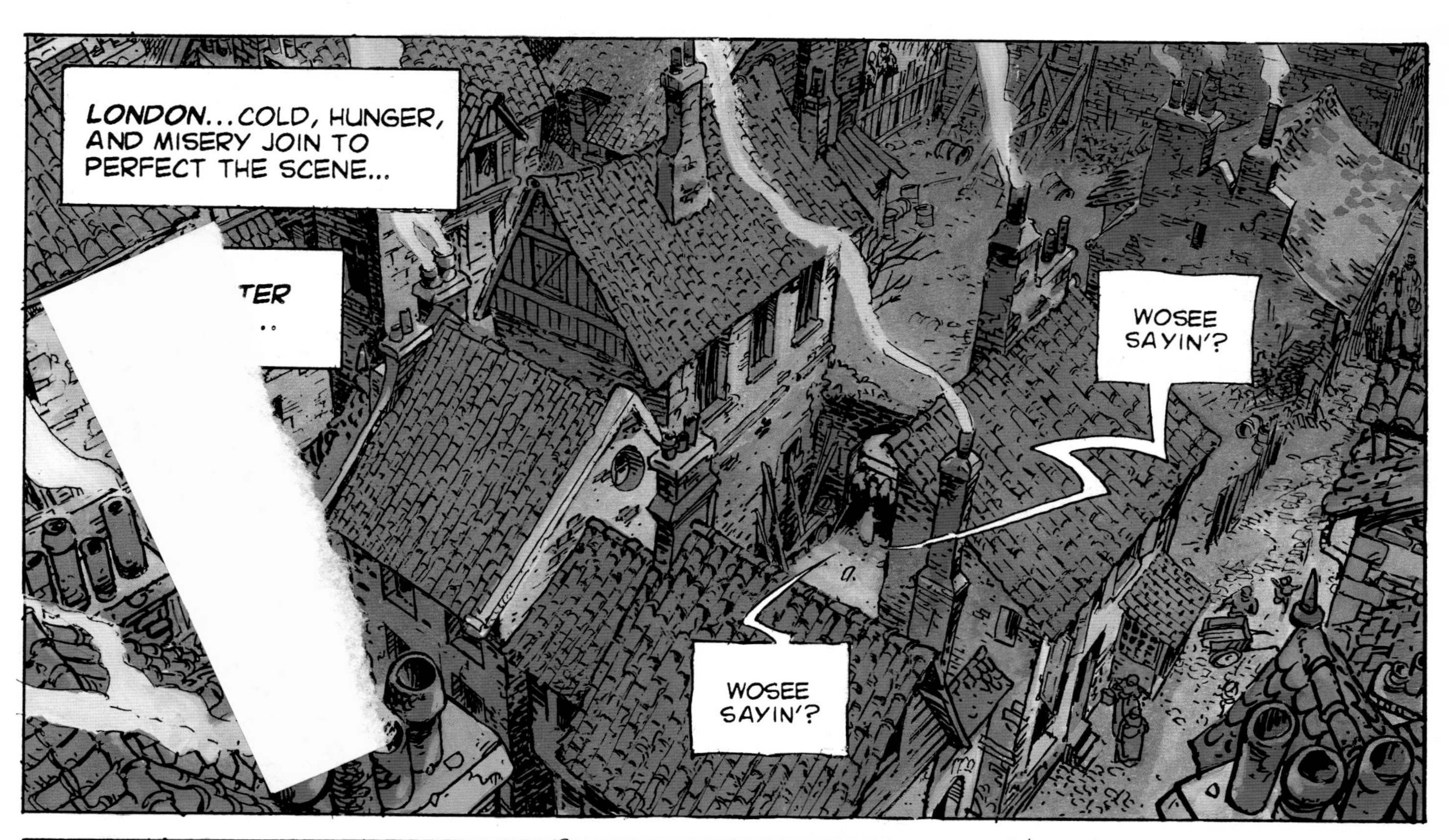
LONDON... COLD, HUNGER, AND MISERY JOIN TO PERFECT THE SCENE...
WOSEE SAYIN'?
WOSEE SAYIN'?

...UH? LISSEN, CHAPS-- WOSEE SAYIN', THEN?
'E SEZ YORRA PAIN INNA NECK, PIGSKIN!! GE' BACK T'Y'R POST!

PISS OFF! FIRST UV ALL, THERE'S NO ROOM! AN' SE-COND, Y'R TOO HEAVY!
'S NO' FAIR! 'M AL'AYS TH' ONE STANDS GUARD!
...BU'...

SHU'UP, YOU TWO! CAN'T 'EAR A FING! ANYWAY, PIGSKIN, YA KNOW WE AL'AYS TELL YA AFTER!
STOP ARGUIN', FATSO! ... M'WARNIN' YA, IF WE GET CAUGHT, Y'R GONNA GE' IT!
YEAH, SURE! BU' I'S AL'AYS FER SUMMA ME SOUP!
BASTIDS!

AND ONCE AGAIN THE BEAUTIFUL CINDERELLA WAS LOCKED UP BY HER HORRIBLE STEP-MOTHER AND HER TWO STEPSISTERS.
POOR FING...
OH, TH' BITCHES!
WOSEE SAY?

HEE HEE! I SAY THAT'S ALL FOR TONIGHT!
THE REST TOMOR-ROW.
AW NO, PETER, YA AL'AYS STOP WHEN I'S GETTIN' GOOD.

RATSKY'S RIGHT! C'MON, THEN, PETER!
ENOUGH, LADS! I'M NOT LIKE THE REST OF YOU--
I'VE A DEAR LITTLE MUM WHO'LL BE GETTING WORRIED ABOUT ME!

OH, YEAH! TELL US AG'IN, PETER, WHA' A DEAR LI'L MUM'S LIKE!
AN' TH' HUGS AN' KISSES, PETER! TELL US ABOU' THA'.
AN'... AN' TH' WORDS AS MAKE YA FEEL ALL WARM
MEOW
2

HMM... IT'S NOT EASY TO TELL.
AND, THEN, I'M NOT EVEN SURE YOU'D UNDERSTAND.
THA'S A'RIGHT, PETER-- WE'LL PRETEND!
EH, CHAPS?

'EY, RATSKY! 'OW COME I CAN'T 'EAR NUFFIN'?
SSHH...'E'S GONNA TELL 'BOUT 'IS MUM!

LET'S SEE, THEN! ... A MOTHER'S AS WARM AS A MITTEN WITHOUT HOLES...
WOSEE SAY?
AND MINE IS PRETTY, TOO... VERY PRETTY.

DAFT STUFF-- FULLA HOLES! HEH HEH-- BU' IS REAL NICE!
PSS! PIGSKIN! THREE SPOONFULS'V Y'R SOUP T'NIGHT AN' I'LL TELL YA ALL!
'S A DEAL, CRIBBS-- BUT Y'GOTTA DO TH' GESTURES, TOO!

WHEN SHE COMES TO ME, SO SOFTLY, TO TELL ME SHE LOVES ME...

THE WORDS SHE WHISPERS ARE LIKE A SWEET SCENT THAT MAKES MY HEAD LIGHT AND MY HEART FIT TO BURST...

MEOW.. MEOW..
HER LITTLE HANDS ARE MADE FOR STROKING, AND HER EYES FOR TENDERNESS...
3

AND WHEN SHE COMES INTO MY ROOM FOR THE LA
'IS ROOM...Y'KNOW --F'TH'GOO'NIGHT KISS...
SHIT! WILL YA LOOK A'ME, PIGSKIN! M'DOIN' TH' GES-TURES F'YA!
MEOW
THEN SHE HOLDS ME CLOSE...
...AND IN A VOICE SOFT AS A FEATHER, SHE TELLS ME A BEA-UTIFUL STORY.
MEOW...
AAAH... KEEP GOIN', STUMPS! MAKES ME FEEL GOOD ALL OVER...!

AND THEN, AS MY EYES FLUTTER SHUT, COMFORTED BY SO MUCH LOVE, MY MUM VERY... SOFTLY... STOPS...
PRRR... Prr...
SCRITCH! SCRATCH. SCRATCH.

'E SURE KNOWS 'OW T'TELL 'EM.
SHE TUCKS ME IN, AND THEN...VERY DELICATELY, PLANTS A KISS ...SWEET AS HONEY, SOME-TIMES VANILLA ...ON THE FOREHEAD OF HER DEAR CHILD...
RR RR
RR
ME!...

'EY! SOM'UN'S COMIN'!!

YEAH!S' ONE-ARM JIM!
EV'RYONE INTA THE SHED!
4

?! O.K.--
CURTAIN!
I THINK OUR AUDIENCE HAS ABANDONED US!
SHIIIT!... IT'S HIM A'RIGHT! ONE-ARM JIM! SCRAMBLE, QUICK!

GE' READY, LADS! 'E DON'T LIKE US 'ANGIN' 'ROUN' 'IS RUBBISH!
ONE-ARM, ONE-ARM.

!
WELL, WELL!
WE'D BETTER GO THEN, RIGHT, CAT?
HUP!
MEOW?
SO, YA LI'L BUGGERS! PLAYIN' WITH Y'RSELVES, EH?
GO!

!?
ONE-ARM, ONE-ARM! FACE'D CAUSE A' ALARM!

FILTHY SHIT-HEADS!!
IF I CATCH ONE UV YA, I'LL TEAR 'IS ARMS OFF!!
ONE-ARM
ONE-ARM
CAN'T DO NO 'ARM!
5

RIGHT.
BYE, CAT... THANKS! YOU WERE PERFECT!

GONE... WHEW!! THA' WAS CLOSE!
NO! NO! NO MORE GAMES!
YOU STAY HERE!
MEOW!

PETER...? S'ME--PIGSKIN!
HEE HEE! THEY ALL RAN AWAY LIKE A FLOCK O' SPARROWS!

SHOO!
SHOO!
GET OUT OF HERE, I SAID!
GAME'S OVER!!

BUT... I'M 'ERE, PETE... T-TELL ME... WOT YA SAID, 'BOUT, 'BOUT A MUM?
PETER? YA THERE?
?
PETE--

MEOW!
OH, A LI'L CAT... WOT YA DOIN' 'ERE ALL ALONE?

YA 'UNGRY? YA COLD? LOST Y'R MUM?
DON'T WORRY, C'M'ERE! YOU'LL SEE, I'LL MAKE A MUM UP FOR YA,
C'MON, THEN!
C'MON!
MEOW!

286...
287...
288...

...PETER! PEETERRR...

291..
EH!? EVENING, MR. KUNDAL.

PETER, HOW MANY TIMES MUST I TELL YOU THAT THIS IS YOUR HOME!

BUT I WAS FOLLOWING YOUR ADVICE, MR. KUNDAL...
I WAS COUNTING!

ALL RIGHT, ALL-RIGHT...IT KEEPS YOUR MIND BUSY, BUT IT'S NO REASON TO GO FORGETTING TO EAT!

BUT...
ENOUGH, CHILD! COME EAT BEFORE YOUR SUPPER GETS COLD!

PAPA.. I'M 'UNGRY
LE' I' BE, CHILD-- THINK ABO' Y'R FEET!

'S ONE-ARM JIM! TH' USUAL--A LARGE UN?
YEAH, RIPLEY... ME USUAL!
THE SOUP IS GOOD, EH, PETER...? EAT CHILD! EAT UP!
WHERE DID WE LEAVE OFF YESTERDAY?
SLURP!... WHERE, CINDERELLA IS ALONE, SLURP! ... LOCKED UP.
YES, THAT'S RIGHT... BY THE WAY, DO YOU KNOW ANY GREEK MYTHOLOGY?
NO... SLURP! WHAT'S THAT? A CAKE?
HMM? NO MATTER! SO-- CINDER-ELLA!
TELL ME, RIPLEY--EVER SINCE I BEEN COMIN' 'ERE, I AL'AYS SEES 'AT KID WITH TH' OLD MAN...
HIS GRAND-SON?
NO, BUT HE MIGHT AS WELL BE!

MERMAID TAVERN
F'R TH' SIX YEARS I BEEN 'ERE, I AL'AYS SEEN HIM--BIT TOO MUCH, T'MY TASTE, BU' THA'S NONE O'ME BUSINESS...
EVEN IF TH' OLD FELLA FEEDS HIM BETTER'N ALL TH' REST O' US!
AN' WHEN 'E'S NOT FEEDIN' 'IM, 'E'S FILLIN' 'IS MISERABLE SKULL WITH STUPID STORIES!

AN' THE BEST YET IS THA' BETWEEN ALL THIS FOOLISHNESS, 'E'S MANAGED T'TEACH TH' TYKE T'READ AN' WRITE-- EVEN T'COUNT!
YOU WATCH! SOON TH' OL' COOT'LL BE CASTIN' ME ASIDE FOR THA' INEXPERIENCED KID!
GLOOOGLE

PEGGY! A DOUBLE HELPING OF PUDDING-- AND A LEMONADE!

"A LEMONADE, PEGGY" AN' "A DOUBLE 'ELPIN', PEGGY." PEGGY ME ARSE!! AN' 'ERE I AM, 'AVIN' T'WORK ME ARSE OFF ALL NIGHT FER JUS' ATASTE O' WHUT THA' KID EATS!
I WONDER WHA' 'E SEES IN THA' LI'L SHIT...
YEESSS...
8

MEBBE 'E GOES F'R TH' LI'L DARLIN'S!
PFFF! HEE HEE!
ah! ah ah!

?
HEE HEE HEE!

'ERE, DARLIN'! HEE HEE!
THANK YOU, PEGGY... WHAT HAS YOU CACKLING AWAY LIKE THAT?

MIAM! MACH!
OH, NUFFIN', NUFFIN', MR. KUND'L, SIR! JUS' THINKIN' S'ALL! HEE HEE!

FROM THE LOOK, IT WAS NOT AN INNOCENT THOUGHT.
A GROWN-UP'S IMAGINATION IS THE VERY WORST KIND! LET'S GO.
AN-OTHER, RIPLEY. HA HA!

... LOOK AT THIS WEATHER! IT WAS TO BE EXPECTED!
SEE YOU TOMORROW, SON--AND DON'T DALLY!
YOUR MOTHER MAY BE WORRIED..
HA HA! OF COURSE, MR. KUNDAL, OF COURSE.

BRR! THIS TIME IT'S REALLY COLD! THE SNOWFLAKES ARE BIG ENOUGH TO CLOTHE THE POOR!
ALL RIGHT, START AGAIN, START AT 292...
293

...BRR... WELL, ME GIRL, IF YA DON'T GE' 'EM INSIDE QUICK, THEY'LL FREEZE ON TH' SPOT!

...529 ...530... 531... 532...

WHA?
53
HUH?

YA FOOL! CAN'T YA WATCH--
SORRY, MA'AM!
WELL, WELL! IF IT AIN'T LI'L PETER!
MMM... LE'S 'AV A LOOK, THEN... Y'VE GROWN, Y'HAVE! ALMOST A MAN, PETER!

AN' I'S SO TERRIBLY COLD!
Y- YES... SO?

SO? SO... WOULDN'T YA LIKE MUMSY T' WARM YA UP...?
EH, ME BABY?

!?
LOOKEE, LI'L UN--FEEL 'OW WARM IT IS!

C'MON, GREEDY, DON'T ACT TH' KID!
SUCK 'EM! F'YOU, I'S FREE!

AH! AH! AH!
GROWN UP! GROWN UP! DIRTY GROWN UP!
10

LI'L BASTID ...!

HIC! YEAH... JUS' LIKE 'IS FATHER!

HE'D SHIT IN Y'HAND AN' Y'D STILL 'AVE T'SAY THANK YOU! LAY-ABOUT! HIC! VERMIN!

AN'--VERMIN! I... HIC! I SQUASH 'EM UNDER ME 'EEL!
SLOW COACH!

N... NEVER THERE WHEN I NEED 'IM... I...

I'M HERE... MUM...

...!

TSS! TSS! NO, CHILD...
NO...

PU' I' BACK ON, ANGEL... I'... I'S SO COLD...
AN' Y'POOR MUM... WOULD JUS' LOVE T'GET WARM...
REALLY-- WHAT'S GOTTEN INTO THEM TONIGHT?

LO... LOOK, SON...
I'S--HIC! I'S EMPTY...

...WITHOUT WANTIN' T'FORCE YA--AN' I' MIGHT BE FUN F'R YA... WOULD Y'GO FETCH ME A LI'L BOTTLE--HIC! F'Y'DEAR MUM--HIC! LIKE FUM MIS'ER KUN'L'S, HMM...?
BUT, MUM...

!! DON' CHOO ARGUE!
?! BUT I--

DON' ARGUE!
GO!

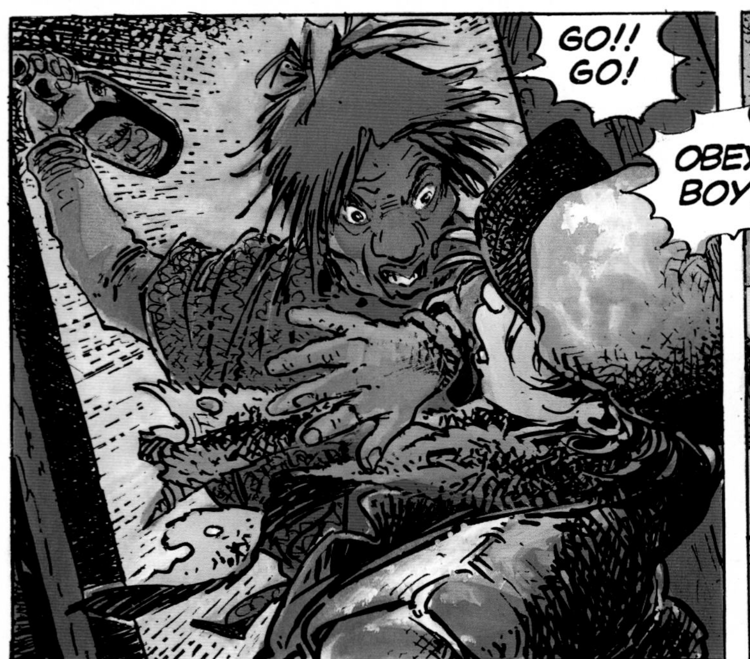
GO!! GO!
OBEY, BOY!

SCHLING!

VLAM!

...BUT...
BUT WHAT DO I BUY IT WITH?

WITH YER ARSE!!

IF Y' COME BACK WITHOUT THA' BOTTLE,
I'LL KILL YA!!
UNNER--STAN'?!

I'LL KILL YA!
VLAM!

...1...2...
3...4
...5...
13

...207...
208...
HELLO THERE, "LOST BOYS."

CHILDREN'S HOSPICE
DREAM... DREAM ON, MY FRIENDS..

THEIR KISSES ARE SO MUCH MORE REAL IN DREAMS..
THE... BITCH!

BITCH!
STOP, PETER! STOP THINK-ING ABOUT IT! 210... 211..

HAVE YOU SOME-THING TO SHOW ME FOR THESE THREE COINS, MY SWEET?
...298 ...299 ...3..

CERTAINLY, GOV'! F'THAT PRICE Y'CAN EVEN POKE Y'BIG NOSE IN! HA HA!
HEE HEE! IT WAS FREE FOR ME! OH, YES-- CHARM! CHARM!
C'MON, WOLFIE! I'LL GIVE YA Y'MONEY'S WORTH!

I HATE YOU!
14

ONE DAY, I'LL GO AWAY...
LIKE MY FATHER.

I HATE HER!

GOOD EVENING, MR. RIPLEY. IS MR. KUNDAL IN?
'E'S OUT! WHA' YA WANT WITH TH' OLD MAN?

TO BORROW... A B-BOTTLE OF... BRANDY ...PLEASE...
NO LESS! 'E A'READY FEEDS YA AN' Y'WANT Y'DRINK, TOO, DO YA?!

WELL! LOOKEE WHO'S 'ERE!
AIN'T 'E A DARLIN'..
...THIS 'ERE MAN?

'E'S NOT LIKE TH' REST O' YA!
I BET 'E'S GOT SOME VIGOR INSIDE JUS' WAITIN' T'GET OUT, EH?
YOU... ?!

HA!
HA!
HA!
HA! HA!
YEAH, KID-- WE'D LIKE T'SEE Y'BIT O' VIGOR, WE WOULD!

FUNNY--BUT Y'R NOT GETTIN' AWAY LIKE THA', ME DARLIN' ...TWO SHILLIN'S AN' I'S YOURS!
I H-HAVE NO MONEY! WHERE'S MR. KUNDAL?

!
'E'S PROB'LY UP 'ERE, BABY! AKE A LOOK...
I'S ITCHY!
MEBBE 'E'S STILL STUCK THERE! HEE HEE!

HA!
HA!
HA!
TH' CUNT! SHE'S GONNA MAKE US PAY F'THA' SHOW!!
'COURSE! AN' MEBBE WE C'D PAY F'R 'IS BOTTLE! 'E'S GOT SUMFIN' T'SHOW US, TOO, EH, LADS?

YEAH! I'LL PUT DOWN A PENNY!
I'S A DEAL! ONE-ARM JIM GIVE A PENNY.
WHO'S NEXT?
GLING!
GLING!
16

TWO PENCE!
FIVE PENCE! HA HA!
'ERE'S THREE PENCE MORE!
A PENNY F'ME!
ONE SHILLIN... AN' THREE PENCE, 7 AN' 6 PENCE... 8... 9...

THREE PENCE FUM ME AN' 'E'S GOT IT!
Y'R TURN! I'S ALL Y'RS!
BRANDY
CHOC!
DIGLING!

OH, YES-- YA PAY F'EVERYTHIN', DARLIN'! HA HA HA!
MUM...
I HATE YOU! I HATE YOU! I HATE YOU! I HATE YOU! I HATE YOU! I--

HUP THERE! UP ON TH' COUNTER, KID, SO'S EVERYONE C'N SEE YA!
!!

PETER, YOU MUST,
WATCH OUT, GIRLS!
HA!
YOU MUST HAVE THAT BOTTLE...

A-TEN-SHUN! 'E'S UNWRAPPIN' TH'GOODS!!

HA!
HA!
HA!
HA!
WELL, WELL! SOM'UN'S BEEN TELLIN' LIES! I'S NONE TOO VIGOROUS, 'IS THING!!
HA!

I'S JUS' TH' EXCITEMENT, EH, BABY?...'ERE! 'E'S WON 'IS BOTTLE!
DON'T WORRY, ME PET. MUMSY'LL FIX THAT!
MMM...BEND DOWN! I'LL PROVE 'EM WRONG!

HA!
HA!
HA!
HA!
HA!
HA HA! THA'S IT-- RUN AWAY!
AN' WHEN Y'R BIGGER, COME SEE ME! BUT DON'T FORGET--NEXT TIME, YOU'LL BE PAYIN'! HEE HEE HEE!

PETER! STOP! IT'S ME!
?
!? MISTER KUNDAL!!
I'M SORRY ...I SAW EVERY-THING, MY BOY.

AND YOU DIDN'T STOP THEM?

YOUR MOTHER?
YES...

SHE WOULD'VE KILLED ME, MR. KUNDAL... KILLED ME...
COME...

S'LONG, ONE-ARM JIM!
SEE YA... T'MORROW, RIPLEY-- HIC!
18

HOW LONG HAVE WE KNOWN EACH OTHER, PETER?
FOREVER, MR. KUNDAL, FOREVER...
YES, 13 YEARS ALREADY, DON'T GROW UP TOO QUICKLY...

I DON'T WANT TO GROW UP! NEVER! NEVER!
THEN KEEP AWAY FROM "THE GREAT DEVOURER."

? "THE GREAT DEVOURER"?
TIME, MY BOY! TIME!

HE WANTS SOMETHING, HE TAKES IT, SWALLOWS IT. EVERYTHING ENDS UP BELONGING TO HIM-- EVEN THE LITTLE BOX BURIED AT THE BOTTOM OF YOUR HEART.
IMAGINE A LITTLE CANDY BOX THAT CONTAINS ONLY A SINGLE PIECE OF CANDY...

A FABULOUS CANDY THAT WOULD TASTE LIKE A DREAM, FLAVORED WITH ADVENTURE AND WRAPPED IN IMAGINATION!

BUT TIME IS MERCILESS AND TENACIOUS --IT KNOWS PATIENCE! IT WORRIES THE BOX AND TOSSES IT ABOUT EVERY WHICH WAY...

THE CANDY BOUNCES AROUND AND FALLS OUT! THEN "THE GREAT DEVOURER" TAKES IT AWAY, AND... SLOWLY... EATS...IT.

THERE...TIME HAS PASSED. THE BOX IS STILL THERE, BUT THE FABULOUS CONTENT IS GONE. INSIDE, THE OLD WRAPPER-- YELLOWED WITH AGE--LIES ALONE, REMEMBERING WITH A FAINT SMILE HAVING SHARED THE MOST WONDERFUL STORY WITH HIS FRIENDS, THAT OF HAVING ONCE BEEN A CHILD!
THAT MAY BE THE PURPOSE OF GROWING OLD... REMEMBERING THAT ONCE YOU WERE A CHILD...

I AM A CHILD! A CHILD! A CHILD! AND THE GREAT DEVOURER CAN'T DO ANYTHING ABOUT IT!

THAT'S NOT ENOUGH, PETER. YOU MUST WANT IT, BUT YOU MUST ESPECIALLY BELIEVE IT!! BELIEVE IN THE POWER OF THE IMAGINATION.
LET'S SIT DOWN, PETER.
19

PETER... LET'S TALK ABOUT YOUR FATHER, SHALL WE?
!? MY FATHER!

YES. I CAN TELL YOU NOW--I KNEW HIM WELL WHEN HE WAS ABOUT YOUR AGE...
YOU KNEW HIM?! HOW ABOUT THAT! WHY DID YOU NEVER TELL ME?

BAH! I WAS WAITING FOR THE RIGHT MOMENT! THERE'S A TIME FOR EVERYTHING, LITTLE ONE... AND I SUPPOSE YOU'VE ASKED YOUR MOTHER ABOUT HIM?
YES, BUT YOU KNOW WHAT SHE'S LIKE! SH...SHE...
WELL, I AVOID BRINGING IT UP...

WH...WHAT WAS HE LIKE?
OH, NOTHING LIKE YOU! BUT YOU DO HAVE SOMETHING IN COMMON--THE STORIES!
--AND THE DREAMS THEY LEAD TO!
HE CAME FROM A VERY RICH FAMILY. ...ONE DAY, HIS PARENTS PERISHED IN A SHIPWRECK. IT WAS A TERRIBLE BLOW TO HIM, BUT HE SUFFERED MOST THE LOSS OF HIS MOTHER.

HMPH! MINE NEVER GETS INTO BOATS --PITY!!
HEE HEE! BLESSED CHILD!

FROM THEN ON, THE POOR BOY BECAME EVER MORE SOMBER AND GLOOMY... HIS ENTIRE CHILDHOOD WAS FILLED WITH TUTORS, TEACHERS, GOVERNESSES...

HIS FATHER HAD ALWAYS WANTED HIS SON TO BE IMPORTANT, BUT HIS SON DREAMED OF ONLY ONE THING...
THE SEA!

AS SOON AS HE WAS ABLE, HE CAME DOWN TO THE QUAYS AND DAYDREAMED NEAR THE BIG SHIPS...
HERE HE HAD PRO-BABLY HIS GREATEST ADVENTURES!

THAT'S HOW I... NOTICED HIM, HERE ON THE QUAY. AT THE TIME, I WORKED ON THE DOCKS.
WE USED TO MEET REGULARLY, TO TALK OF THE GREAT MYSTERIES OF THE SEA, OF--
NAVIGA-TORS?! SEA MONSTERS?! PI--PIRATES, TOO?! TREASURE, AND--
YES, PETER, YES! ALL OF THAT!
20

YES...THAT'S ALL HE THOUGHT OF-- LEAVING!
IT WAS A...A SICKNESS WITH HIM...HE DIDN'T HAVE ANY FRIENDS. HE'D BECOME A HARD AND TOUCHY YOUNG MAN.

AND WHEN HE CAME OF AGE AND INHERITED HIS FORTUNE, HE TOOK IT INTO HIS HEAD TO BUY A SHIP.

BUT THEN ONE DAY HE MET A WOMAN WHO WAS TO UPSET HIS PLANS FOR A WHILE--YOUR MOTHER!
M-MUM.

COME NOW, PETER --FORGET THAT! SOMETIMES WE MUST CLIMB ONTO THE DEVIL'S BACK TO GET WHAT WE WANT!

LONDON DOESN'T GIVE THE UNFORTUNATE MUCH CHOICE, AND PEOPLE LIKE YOUR MOTHER CAN SOMETIMES BE ...VERY... CONVINCING.
!?
'OW 'BOUT A LI'L TREAT, DARLIN'?

THAT LEFT ONLY LUCK, THE RIGHT NUMBER...SHE GOT IT--AND SHE WAS DETERMINED TO KEEP IT!
!?
BEAT IT!!

AND THE SIMPLEST WAY TO KEEP HIM WAS TO MARRY HIM ...HIM--BUT ESPECIALLY HIS FORTUNE!

SHE KNEW THAT DESPITE HER CHARMS, YOUR FATHER'S PASSION WAS STRONGER ...AND SHE SENSED HER PREY ESCAPING, SO SHE ...ANNOUNCED THAT SHE WAS...EXPECTING HIS BABY...HIS CHILD! YOU!
BAD MOVE! HE LEFT, AND WE NEVER SAW HIM AGAIN.
HMPH! BASTARD!

I HEARD MUCH LATER THAT HIS SHIP HAD SUNK WITH ALL ABOARD, YOUR FATHER, THE CREW...
THERE NOW, PETER...HIS END WAS THE SAME AS HER'S WHOM HE HAD SO LOVED BEFORE...HIS MOTHER.

BAH! KNOWING MY MOTHER, I CAN'T BE MAD AT HIM! AND THEN--
WHO KNOWS? I MIGHT NOT HAVE LIKED HIM ANYWAY!
HOP!
HEH HEH! IT'S TRUE--HE WAS NOT A BARREL OF LAUGHS!
21

AH! I NEARLY FORGOT--I HAVE SOMETHING FOR YOU, SON!
FOR ME?

YOUR FATHER GAVE IT TO ME ONE DAY... NOW THAT YOU CAN READ, MORE OR LESS, I THOUGHT YOU SHOULD HAVE IT.
OH! A BOOK!

YES, A BOOK ON GREEK MYTHOLOGY. YOU SEE--HEH HEH! IT'S NOT A CAKE, BUT WONDERFUL STORIES! HE WAS ESPECIALLY FOND OF THE ONE ABOUT ULYSSES...

ULYSSES...?
HE WAS A LEGENDARY HERO--TOO LONG TO GO INTO NOW, SOMETHING ABOUT A LONG SEA JOURNEY.

ULYSSE'S ODYSSEY
BUT IF HE LOVED THIS BOOK SO MUCH, WHY DID HE GIVE IT TO YOU?
I DON'T KNOW. I STILL REMEMBER HIS EXPRESSION...

BIZARRE, AS IF THE PAGES BURNED HIS FINGERS.
BAH! AS I SAID, YOUR FATHER SOMETIMES BEHAVED IN THE STRANGEST WAY...
KEEP THE BAG--IT WILL HELP KEEP IT SAFE.

WELL...IT'S GETTING LATE...HERE'S YOUR BOTTLE--AND WATCH OUT FOR YOURSELF, LITTLE ONE.
WHEN YOU'VE CLIMBED ONTO THE DEVIL'S BACK, YOU'RE NOT AFRAID OF ANYTHING ANY MORE! HEH!

THANKS FOR EVERYTHING!
AND SOON I'LL BE THE ONE TELLING YOU STORIES! SEE YOU TOMORROW, MR. KUNDAL!

YES, THAT'S IT--TOMORROW, PETER. TOMORROW...
22

A BOOK--A BOOK FULL OF STORIES! WON'T THE BOYS BE PLEASED!
HEY! HELLO, RATS!
TONIGHT WE CELE-BRATE!
CARE FOR A LITTLE BALLAD ON THE FLUTE?
SQUEAK!
SQUEE!

NOW DON'T WORRY--I'M NOT LIKE THAT OTHER PIPER...
I WON'T DROWN YOU, I PROMISE! HEE HEE!

HERE GOES, MY RODENTS! COME ON--DANCE TO THE MUSIC!
SQUEE!
SQUEAK...
SQUEAK!
SQUEE...

?
HUH? WHERE'VE THEY GONE? HOW STRANGE! THEY FOLLOWED IN THE STORY! HMF! LACK OF TRUST, THAT!

WHEW!
TREAT A DONKEY WITH KINDNESS AND HE'LL SURELY KICK YOU.
CRAC!

WHAT TH--?

BAH!...
PROBABLY SOME DOG CHASING THE RATS...
23

SQUEAK!
SQUEAK!

SQUEAK!!

GROUA!
SQUEE!
SQUEAK!

THERE! JUST AS I THOUGHT!
DOGS! I KNOW A FEW FURRY FELLOWS IN FOR A NASTY QUARTER OF AN HOUR!
GRAOW!
WAW!
WAW!

YOU TOO, MR. BRANDY, YOU TOO! YOUR MINUTES ARE NUMBERED!
HA HA! YOU'LL SEE --YOU WON'T BE LONG IN MOTHER'S COMPA--
NEEARK !?

QUIET, ME DARLIN', QUIET! I WON'T 'ARM YA!

QU--QUITE TH'OPPOSITE, EH? HA HA!
UH! UH! M-MY BOTTLE!

Y'R BOTTLE!? Y'R BOTTLE?! I PAID F'R IT, AN' I DIN'T GET ME MONEY'S WORTH, EH?
I... I... R-RECOGNIZE YOU FROM THE INN! ONE-ARM JIM! L-LET ME GO! YOU...YOU'RE DRUNK!

YEAH, LI'L WHORE-SON, I'M DRUNK-- WELL DRUNK! HAR! I SEES TWO O' YA-- AN' I' TURNS ME ON, SEE?
DOUBLY! HAR HAR!

YA LIKE MUSIC, EH, LI'L UN? LOOK A' ME BIG FLUTE!
SURE AN' YOU'LL LIKE IT, ME CUTIE!
GO ON AN' PLAY!

GROAW
PLAY!
SQUEAK
SQUEE
SQUEAK

WRÖF!
SQUEE!
SQUEE!
25

EH--
WHAA!?!
SQUEAK...
SQUEE!
SQUEAK!
SQUEE!

GRO
SQUEAK...
SQUEE...
GRO

SQUEAK!
SQUEE...
GET OFF,
VERMIN!

OFF!
OFF!
DIRTY
CURS!
SQUEAK...
SQUEAK!
SQUEE!
GRROWWL!

! MY
BOTTLE!

K-KID,
HELP ME!
QU...
QUICK! A...
S-STICK...
SQUEAK
SQUEE
DIE,
PIG-
FACE!!

HUH! HUH!
COME BACK!
NOOOOAAAAHH!
SQUEAK!
GRR

THAT'S IT,
PIGFACE! HEE HEE!
ONE-ARM CAN'T
DO NO
HARM!
26

HEE HEE...! UH-OH! WATCH OUT-- SLIPPERY!
ALMOST THERE, MR. BRANDY, AND NOW'S NO TIME TO BREAK YOUR NECK!

ROWF! ROWF!
?!? NOO!

MUM! MUM!

MOVE IT, PETER, MOVE IT, OR HE'LL TEAR YOU TO PIECES!!

HELP ME, MUM! HELP ME!
WROOGRR

HE'S COMING!! MUM! MUM! QUICK! OPEN THE DOOR!

!?
THE DOO--

GRR...!!

YIPE!
YIPE!
YIPE!
YIPE!!
AARH! ME BOTTLE!

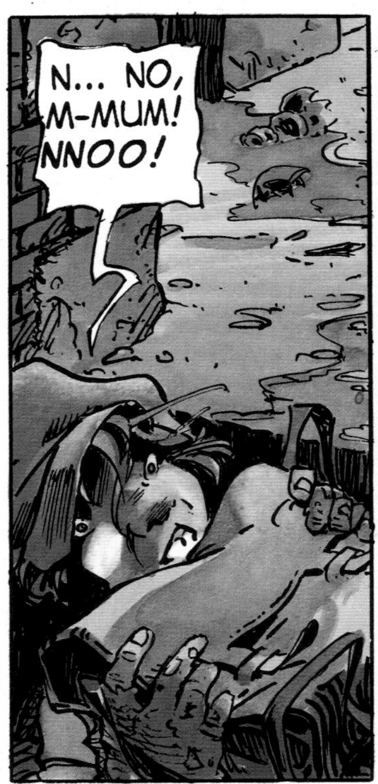
N... NO, M-MUM! NNOO!

VLACH!
VLACH!
ME BO...BOTTLE! YA DID I' ON PURPOSE, YA DIRTY BASTID!

SLAM!

STOP, MUM! YOU'RE MAD! YOU'RE--

MAD!
UGH!
SLAP!

SHIT!
I'LL KILL YOU! YA HEAR? I'LL... KILL YA...
M... ME BOTTLE... UHN... ME BO...TTLE...
28

HOU!
HOU!

HOU!
HOU!

HOU!
HOU!
HOU!

FLAP!
FLAP!
FLAP!

NO, WISE OWL...
NO SINGING TONIGHT...
HOU!
HOU!
HOU!

MY FLUTE IS BROKEN, AND I'M IN TATTERS.
Hou!
YES, *WISE OWL,* I'M EXILED AGAIN...
AND THIS TIME, I THINK IT'S FOR A LONG WHILE.

BUT I'M GLAD YOU'RE WITH ME, WISE OWL.
I MAY BE SORE, HUNGRY, BUT THE COMPANY OF A FRIEND REKINDLES THE SPIRIT.
Hou!

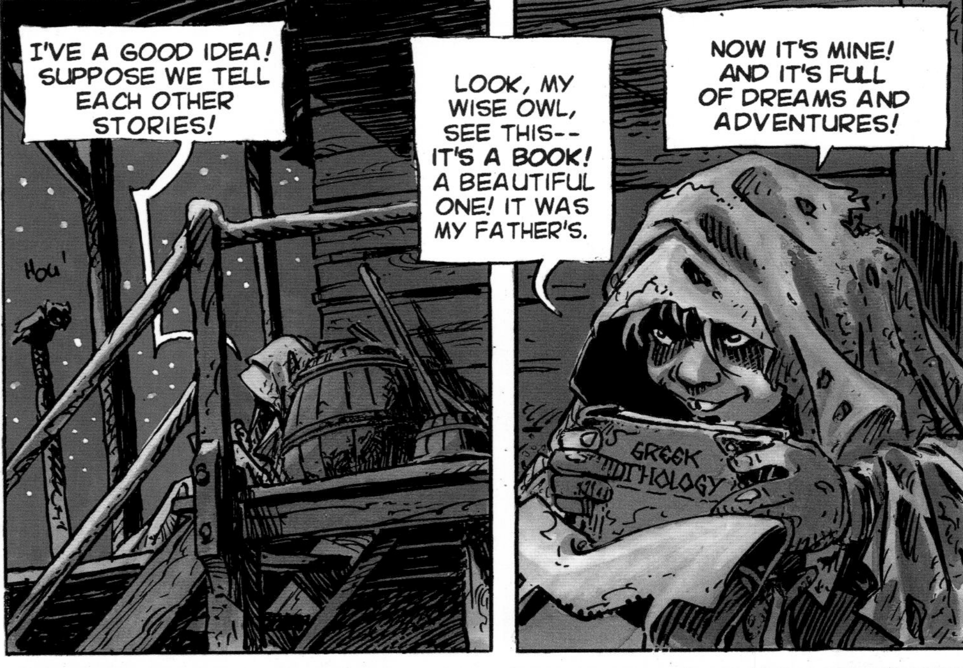
I'VE A GOOD IDEA! SUPPOSE WE TELL EACH OTHER STORIES!
Hou!
LOOK, MY WISE OWL, SEE THIS-- IT'S A *BOOK!* A BEAUTIFUL ONE! IT WAS MY FATHER'S.
NOW IT'S MINE! AND IT'S FULL OF DREAMS AND ADVENTURES!
GREEK

LISTEN, NOW... I'LL READ YOU SOMETHING...
Hou!
...AT RANDOM, MMM... IN AN... ANCIENT CITY L... *LIVED* A LITTLE...
...BOY WITH HIS... MOTHER. HIS N... *NAME* WAS... TH... THE... SE.. US. HIS GRAND-FATHER RULED THIS COUNTRY... HIS MOTHER'S NAME...

...NEVER SAW...? LISTEN, OWL! HE NEVER SAW HIS FATHER--LIKE ME!
O.K.! I'LL GO ON!
SO, SHE--?
30

I SAW YOU, OWL! YOU'RE ASLEEP!
I KNOW I DON'T READ VERY WELL, BUT YOU COULD MAKE AN EFFORT!

OH! LOOK AT ALL THE STARS! THERE'S THOUSANDS OF THEM...
HOU!
IF I HAD WINGS, WISE OWL, I'D FLY FROM STAR TO STAR, FROM ADVENTURE TO ADVENTURE!

HA! WHEN I WAS SMALL, I WANTED TO BE A BIRD... A BIRD WITH GREAT WINGS!
OH! LOOK!
A SHOOTING STAR!

QUICK, MAKE A WISH, OWL!
CLOSE YOUR EYES AND WISH VERY HARD!

! HOU!?
VERY HARD... NNGN...

FLAP!
FLAP!
NNGN ...?

!? HUH? HEY, WHAT DID I SAY, WISE OWL? COME BACK!
31

HA HA! SILLY IDIOT!

DON'T YOU KNOW YOU CAN'T EAT SHOOTING...

...STARS...

..?!

POC!

Hou!
Hou!
Hou!
32

INCREDIBLE! I'VE CAUGHT A SHOOTING STAR!!

WITHOUT ME, YOU'D SURELY HAVE BEEN GOBBLED UP! HEE HEE!
I'M PETER. COME ON-- SHOW YOURSELF.

HEE HEE! DON'T BE AFRAID...
THE WISE OWL IS GONE NOW!

WHA-! HEY, WAIT! DON'T GO!

TINKLE-TINK!
BUT... YOU'RE NOT A STAR!?

FANTASTIC! A... A FAIRY! A TEENSY WEENSY FAIRY!
I KNEW THEY EXISTED, BUT I NEVER THOUGHT...

TH-THEY WERE SO PRETTY.

TINKLE! TINKA!
TLINK!
DING!
TING!
?
HEH! HEY! IS THIS A GAME, ALL THESE GESTURES? I... I HAVE TO GUESS? THAT IT? HEH!

I...I DON'T KNOW WHAT YOU MEAN... HEE HEE!

BUT IT LOOKS SO FUNNY! HEE HEE!

HUNH? UH... ALL RIGHT, O.K --IT'S N-NOT FUNNY!
33

HOW YOU JUMP ABOUT! BUT I STILL DON'T UNDERSTAND ANYTHING!
AND YET, WITH-OUT BOASTING, I AM SORT OF THE INTELLIGENT TYPE...
RIGHT. LET'S START AGAIN FROM THE BEGINNING --MORE... SLOOW-LY.
UN-DER-STAND ?

!AAAHH
WHA-?! AAAAHH! YOU WANT ME TO COME WITH YOU?
UP THERE?

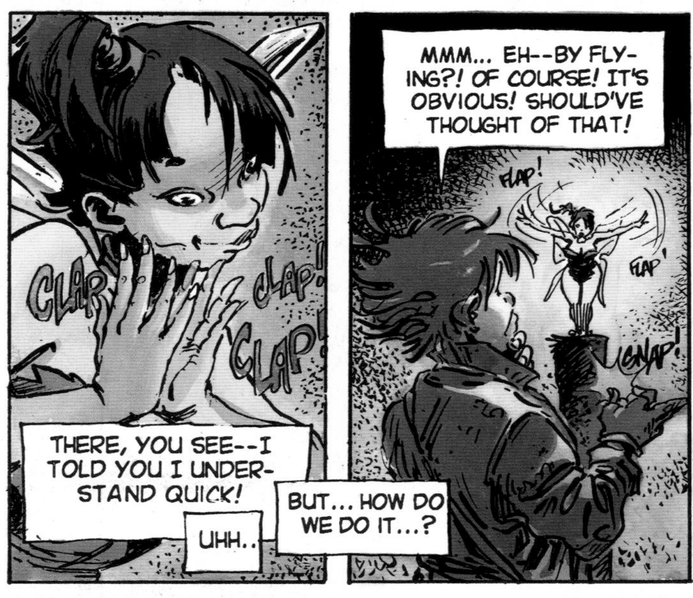
CLAP!
CLAP!
CLAP!
THERE, YOU SEE--I TOLD YOU I UNDER-STAND QUICK!
UHH..
MMM... EH--BY FLY-ING?! OF COURSE! IT'S OBVIOUS! SHOULD'VE THOUGHT OF THAT!
FLAP!
FLAP!
SNAP!
BUT... HOW DO WE DO IT...?

ALL RIGHT. YOU'RE PRETTY SMART FOR A GIRL FAIRY...
FLAP!
FLAP!
FLAP
FLAP
IF I'VE GOT IT RIGHT, ALL I HAVE TO DO IS FLAP MY ARMS AND WANT TO DO IT... AND ESPECIALLY BELIEVE IN IT!
AS MR. KUNDAL WOULD SAY! HEE HEE!

O.K., LET'S GO! I'LL FOLLOW YOU--BUT I'M WARNING YOU...

TINKLE!
TINKLE!
I'M THE BOSS HERE!

HA! PETER, YOU DON'T KNOW WHERE YOU'RE GOING, BUT--HUP! HERE...
34

GOES -- OUCH!
SPLA!

BITCH!
TINK!
TINKLE!
?

SHOULD'VE KNOWN BETTER THAN TO TRUST HER! YOU'RE ALL THE SAME!
YOU LIKE MAKING US SUFFER, EH?
HEE!
YOU THINK IT'S FUNNY?! VERY CLEVER!

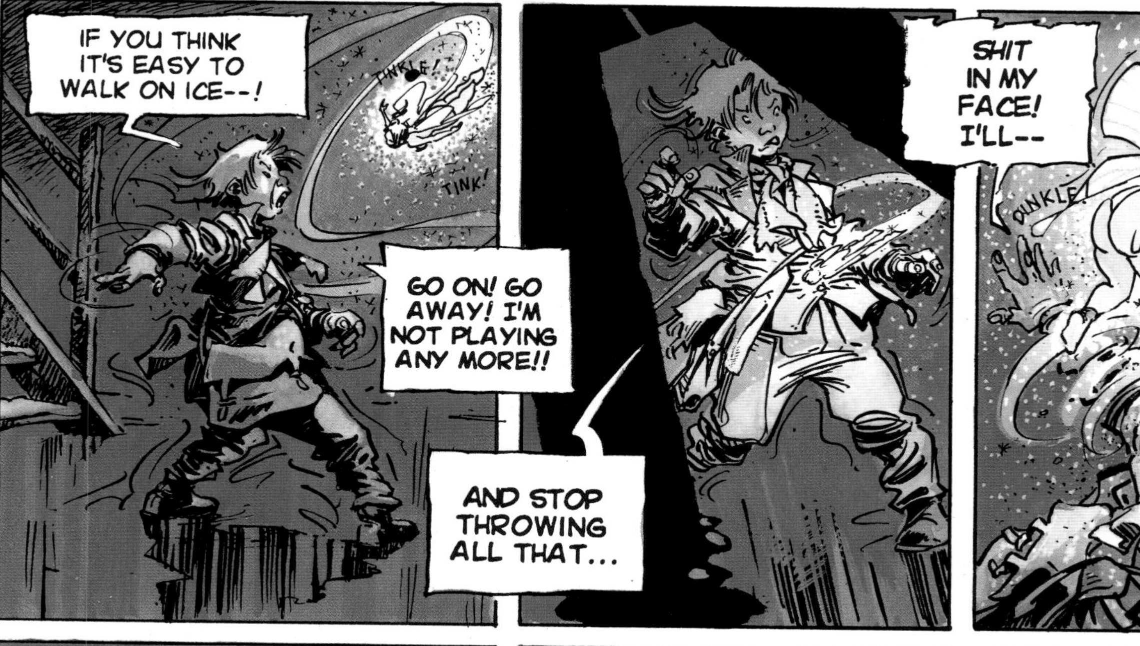
IF YOU THINK IT'S EASY TO WALK ON ICE--!
TINKLE!
TINK!
GO ON! GO AWAY! I'M NOT PLAYING ANY MORE!!
AND STOP THROWING ALL THAT...

SHIT IN MY FACE! I'LL--
TINKLE!
DINKLE!
DLING
TINKLE!

...BREAK MY-- AAH!
DLING!
TINK!
TINKLE!

WHA--?
TINKLE!
DLING!
DINKLE!

I... I... I...
35

I'M FLYING! I'M FLYING...
I CAN DO IT!! HA HA! PETER, YOU'RE TERRIFIC! MARVELOUS! FANTASTIC!
LOOK AT ME! I'M FLYING, GLIDING! I... I'M FANTASTIC!

HEE HEE! SURPRISED YOU, DIDN'T I FAIRY?
TINKLE!
DINKLE!
DLING!

DLING!
?! HEY, WAIT! DON'T BE MAD! IT'S PARTLY THANKS TO YOU...
...PROB-ABLY...

PLEASE, DON'T BE MAD, MISS... MISS DINKLE-DING!
HOU?
YOU'RE SO PRETTY!

IT'S TRUE, YOU KNOW!
IN FACT-- DO YOU LIKE MISS DINKLE-DING FOR A NAME?

EH... GUESS NOT...
36

HEE HEE!
WHAT DO
YOU THINK OF
MRS. JINGLE-
JANGLE?
HMM, NO.
NOT GREAT
... UH...
I'VE
GOT IT!
TINKERBELL!
THE TINKERBELL
FAIRY! MY LITTLE
TINKERBELL FAIRY!

MMM...
I SENSE
YOU LIKE
THAT ONE.
HEE HEE!

INCREDIBLE!
LOOK, TINK--
FROM UP HERE
EVEN POVERTY
LOOKS BEAUTIFUL!
LOOK AT ME!
LOOK AT ME,
EVERYONE!
I CAN FLY!

I'M
FLYIIING!
HA!
TINKLE!
DINKLE!
TINKLE!
DINKLE!

HUFF... PUFF ... UHH... YES, G... GEORGE, GO ON... GO ON... I C'N FLY, TOO! I'M FLYIIIN'...
HUH? WHA-?!

OH, TINK, WAIT! THAT'S WHERE THEY LIVE!

THEY'RE MY FRIENDS-- LET'S VISIT THEM!

CRIBBS! PIGSKIN! THE TWINS!

IT'S ME-- PETER! PSST! STUMPY! LOUSE! LIZARDNECK!
!?

HEY! CHAPS--
GET UP FOR PETE'S SAKE! YOU'LL SEE SOMETHING INCREDIBLE!
TOC!
TOC!

...?
MYOW?
LOOK WHAT YOUR PETER CAN DO!

...PETER?!

DLING!
TLING!
!?
ARRR! YOU'RE HURTING ME, TINK!

WAIT! WAIT! LET GO, I ... HAVE TO...
...SHOW THE BOYS--

THA-AAAH!
DLING!
TINKLE!

PETER...?
...MEOW...

BITCH! WE AGREED I WOULD BE THE LEADER!
UNDERSTAND, TINKERBELL?

D'YA SEE WHA' I SAW, KITTS? TH-THA' WUZ EXTR'ORD'N'RY! TH' BOYS'LL N-NEVER BELIEVE IT, NO WAY!
39

BLOUB!
BLUB!
BLUB!
READY! PREPARE TO DROP ANCHOR!
HE'S COMING UP!

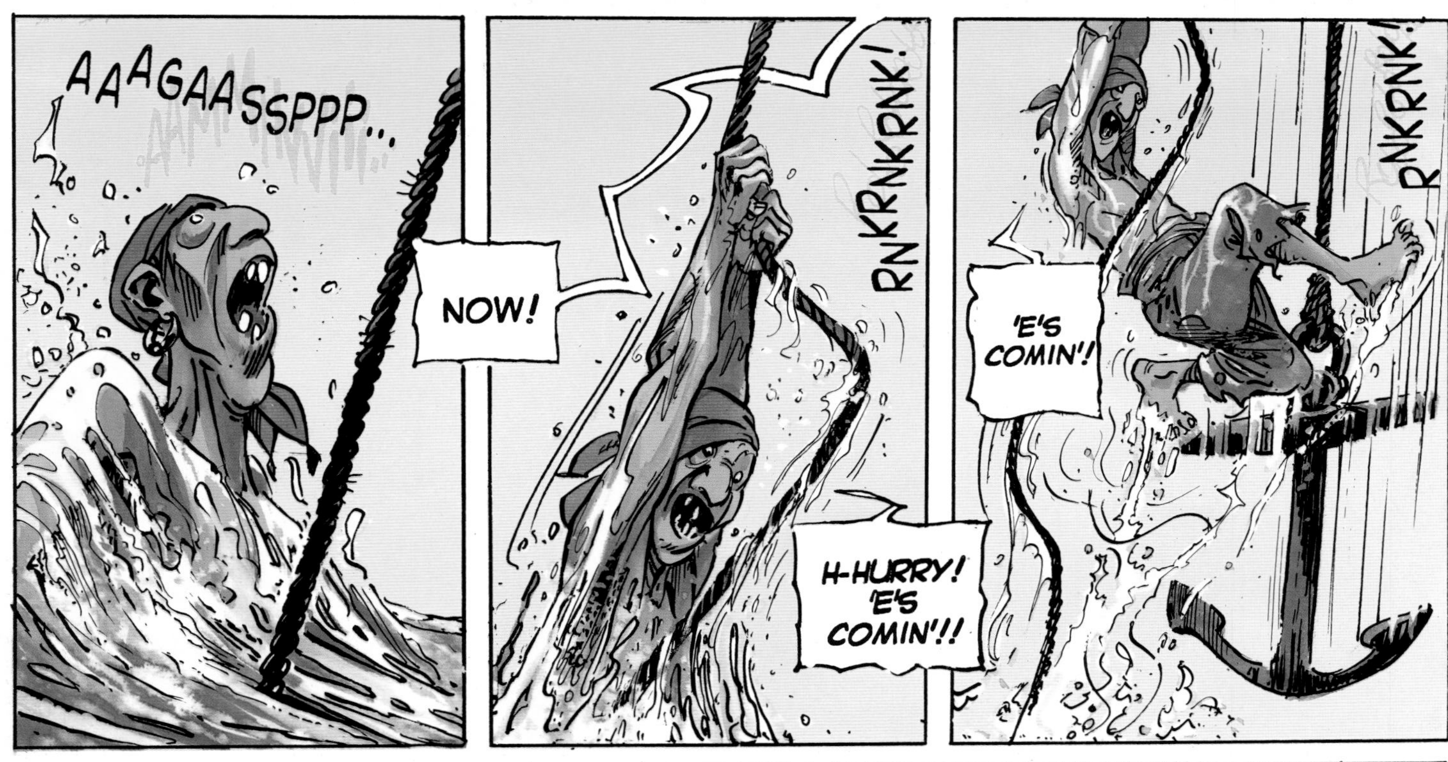
AAAGAASSPPP...
NOW!
RNKRNKRNK!
H-HURRY! 'E'S COMIN'!!
'E'S COMIN'!
RNKRNK!

AAAHR..
RNKRNKR
SPLOF!

..?!
MISSED! MISSED! HE MISSED ME! HA! HA!
SPLACH!
SNAP
40

WELL?
N-N-NO-NOTHIN', C-C-CAP'N! N-NOTHIN'!
C-CAREFUL, LADS! H-HOLD ONTA TH' ROPE! 'E-'E'S ST-STILL THERE!

OF COURSE NOTHING! HE DOESN'T GIVE US TIME!
HUFF! 'AD A LUCKY ESCAPE, BOYO! Y'WERE ALMOS' NUMBER NINE!
CURSÉD CROCODILE! HE'S ALREADY GOBBLED UP EIGHT OF MY MEN!
EIGHT!
AND ALL FOR NOTHING!
I'M FURIOUS!

I WANT THAT TREASURE, YOU HEAR?! INCOMPETENT FOOLS!

CLACK! CLACK!
INCOMPETENT?! INCOMPETENT?! 'AVE YA SEEN THA' CROC?!
I'D LIKE T'SEE YOU DOWN THERE!!

WHAT?
WHAT DID YOU SAY?! REBEL!
ERR...
OOPS

UH... NNNO, C-CAP'N-- A J-JOKE! HA HA!
R-RIGHT, LADDIES?

A JOKE, EH? HA HA HA!
...A-HEH... Y'SEE, CAP'N? Y-YER LAUGHIN'... ERRK...
AYE! AYE! BAD, THAT! VERY BAD!
RRK...Y'SEE...H-HOW GOOD I' F-FEELS T'...T'L-LAUGH?... RKK...
N-NO, CA-CA-CAP'N--Y-YER NOT GONNA HIT A MAN THA'S STILL WE--

WET...
AAARR!

PLÖF!

N--BLBBLBLBBL BLBBLBLBBL NNNOooo RRR AAARRRBLBBLB BBLBLBLB GLUB
NINE!

DAMN CROCODILE! THAT'S NINE OF MY MEN HE'S EATEN!
42

THE RESPONSIBLE ONE IS YOU ALONE! YES, PLUMPINE-- YOU AND NO ONE ELSE!
TO DRAW A SHIP WITH ALL IT'S CREW HERE WITH YOUR SINGING, THAT'S NORMAL, THE NATURE OF A SIREN.

TO HAVE SUCCUMBED TO THEIR CAPTAIN'S CHARM MAKES NO SENSE, BUT WE'LL PASS ON THAT!

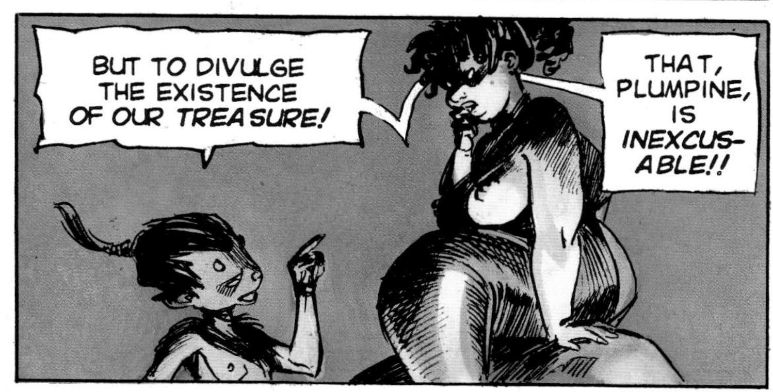
BUT TO DIVULGE THE EXISTENCE OF OUR TREASURE!
THAT, PLUMPINE, IS INEXCUSABLE!!

YES. YOU'RE RIGHT, PAN. SHE'S CONDEMNED THE WHOLE ISLAND WITH THIS FOOLISHNESS!
IT'S YOU, IT'S ME-- YOU'VE EXECUTED ALL OF US!

WELL, LET'S NOT PANIC-- THEY HAVEN'T FOUND OUR TREASURE YET!
THEY MAY NEVER FIND IT!
SNORE
SZZSNORE
ZZZSNORE
THE WATCHMAN WATCHES!

NO, PLUMPINE! IN SUCH CASES, IT'S THE DOUBT THAT'S INTOLERABLE.
SOONER OR LATER, THEIR DEVIL OF A CAPTAIN WILL FIND A SOLUTION!
43

DDRRiii
THAT'S IT! I'VE GOT IT! IT WORKS! IT WORKS! SAURIAN, YOUR DAYS ARE NUMBERED! YOUR DAYS--AND YOUR HOURS HA HA HA HA!
A MERE FEW ADJUSTMENTS, MR. FLEA, AND NOTHING AND NOBODY CAN STOP ME FROM LOOTING THAT TREASURE!
HOW LONG HAS SHE BEEN GONE?

FOR... MM... TWO NIGHTS, IF MEMORY SERVES!
PFF! IT'S SERVES YOU ALL RIGHT-- IT'S WORN OUT! HMM... NO, COUNTING THIS ONE, IT'S... EIGHT NIGHTS...
CERTAINLY NOT! IT'S BEEN 58 NIGHTS! THE PROOF? I COUNTED EACH NIGHT ON MY FINGERS!

BOTH WRONG! SHE'S ONLY BEEN GONE SINCE THIS MORNING!
BUT THAT'S RIDICULOUS! YOU'VE POSITIVELY NO NOTION OF TIME!
IT'S BEEN EXACTLY 128 NIGHTS, AND EIGHT DAYS..

9... 10...11... 12... AND 13! PERFECT! SEE? IT'S SET AT 13 LITTLE MINUTES. HA!
OH NO, CAP'N!! 13'S NO GOOD A NUMBER! I-IT'LL BRING US BAD LUCK, SIR!

HA HA! FLEA, DON'T TELL ME YOU'RE SUPERSTITIOUS!
BEGGIN' Y'R PARDON, CAP'N,
...B-BUT ALL REAL SAIL'RS'RE SUPERTITIOUS!
?! ALL, FLEA? WHAT DO YOU INSINUATE SIRRAH?

THAT I'M NOT A REAL SAILOR, PERHAPS?!
UHN?

EH... Y-YES, YES--I MEAN NO! NO! I MEAN, Y'R A SEAL RAILOR... UH REAL SAILOR! GULP!

GLING!
VRAC
!?
!?
ZBOING!

!?
?!
WHAT THE HELL GOES ON HERE?!
CA... CAP'N, I... I TOLD YOU! S'TH' BEGINNIN' O'TH' BAD LUCK! BAD LUCK!

AAHH, ENOUGH, FLEA! TAKE A CLOSER LOOK AT YOUR BAD LUCK--IT'S NOT EXACTLY THE DEVIL!!
WHEW! THA'S STRANGE!

?... WHAT DID YOU SAY, MR. FLEA?
!!!
EH...GULP...N-NOTHIN', C-CAP'N...I-I WAS SAYIN'...EH...TH-THAT IT'S A STRANGER-- A SP-SPY, IF YA PREFERS...GLUG!

A SPY, YOU SAY? WELL... WELL, WELL, WELL, YOU DO SURPRISE ME, MR. FLEA...
BUT HOW THE DEVIL DID HE GET IN HERE? HMM... INTERRO-GATE HIM, FLEA.
RON... ROONPON
...EH.

Y-YESSIR... BUT THAT'LL BE DIFFI-CULT, CAP'N-- 'E LOOKS EXHAUSTED...
RON... GRRN... GRO.
L-LISTEN-- E'S ASLEEP!

THEN DISCREETLY WAKE HIM, FOOL!

hm? Whazzz ...zzz goin' yaaaawn?
THERE! HE'S AWAKE! THANK YOU, MR. FLEA
Y-Y'R WELC'M, CAP'N!

SO, WHO ARE YOU SPY?
RONRONRON

hnn? Shh...Shut up, basszztard ...can't you szzee 'm tired?...
GRN...
RNAL
!

HEH HEH! INSOLENT, TOO, ISN'T HE? ISN'T THAT SO, MR. FLEA?
C-CERTAINLY, CAP'N! 'E'S NOT VERY POLITE F'R A CHILD...
GRN...
GRN... RON
WILL YA PERMIT ME, CAP'N?

WAKE UP, RIFF-RAFF, AN' EXCUSE Y'RSELF T'TH' CAP'N!
ELSE Y'LL 'AVE ME T'DEAL WITH!
RON
RON...RON...

TSS! TSS! CALM YOURSELF, FLEA. NO NEED TO TERRORIZE HIM! YOU KNOW, MY FRIEND, SOMETIMES YOU'RE A REAL DEMON!
YES, CAP'N, I KNOW. THERE'RE TIMES WHEN I FRIGHTEN M'SELF!
PAT...
PAT...
PAT TAP!
ALLOW ME. I HAVE AN IDEA...

THE ALARM CLOCK. WE'LL TEST IT'S EFFECTIVENESS... HEH HEH! THERE! IT'S SET.
...AND NOW...
CLIC!
TIK...
TIK...TOK...

OBSERVE, MR. FLEA. IT'S AN ABSOLUTE MARVEL...
DRRIIINN

DRRIIINN
WHEN IT RINGS, THE "A" SPRING UNWINDS...AND BY THIS CLEVER PROCEDURE--BY UNWINDING--IT WINDS THE "B" SPRING... SEE--IT WORKS!

AND WHEN THE "B" SPRING IS WOUND, THE ALARM STOPS RINGING... AND 13 MINUTES LATER, THE ALARM GOES OFF AGAIN AS THE "B" SPRING UNWINDS, WHICH IN TURN WINDS THE "A" SPRING-- AND OVER AND OVER AGAIN EVERY 13 MINUTES... THAT'S THE ALTERNATING MOVEMENT! HA HA! ANNOYING, ISN'T IT?

SO! YOU UNDERSTAND THE OBJECTIVE IS TO REVERSE THE DAY AND NIGHT RHYTHMS OF THE CROCODILE.
BUT I MUST PERFECT MY LITTLE SYSTEM SO IT RINGS ONLY AT NIGHT...
46

'F I UNNERSTAND YA CORRECKLY, CAP'N, YA INTEND T'DISTURB TH' NIGHTS O' TH' CROC SO HE SLEEPS ALL DAY, HUH?
AN' OUR DIVERS'LL BE ABLE T'CALMLY RETRIEVE TH' TREASURE!
PRECISELY, FLEA. PRECISELY.

OOH! Y'R DIABOLICAL, CAP'N! DI-A-BOL-I-CAL! AN' WHAT YA 'AVE IN MIND F'R TH' CHILD?

WELL, WE'RE SHORT OF MEN, FLEA... I THINK HE'LL MAKE A SUPERB PIRATE, EH?
OR ELSE A SCRUMPTIOUS MORSEL FOR THE CROC!
OOH! GOOD UN, CAP'N.

NOW, FLEA, LET'S WAIT ANOTHER 13 MINUTES, JUST TO TEST THE SLEEP OF OUR STOWAWAY! HA!

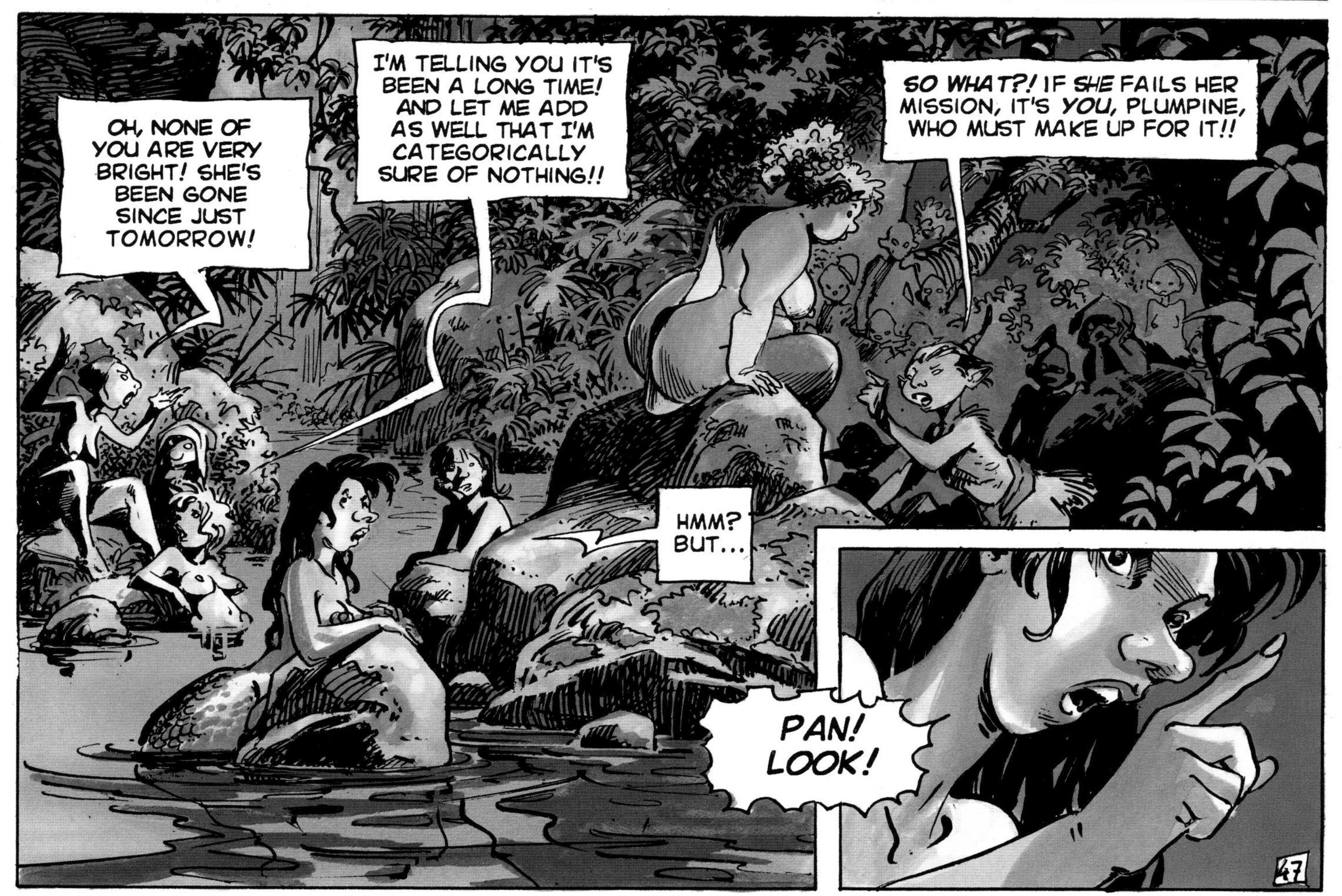
OH, NONE OF YOU ARE VERY BRIGHT! SHE'S BEEN GONE SINCE JUST TOMORROW!
I'M TELLING YOU IT'S BEEN A LONG TIME! AND LET ME ADD AS WELL THAT I'M CATEGORICALLY SURE OF NOTHING!!
SO WHAT?! IF SHE FAILS HER MISSION, IT'S YOU, PLUMPINE, WHO MUST MAKE UP FOR IT!!
HMM? BUT...
PAN! LOOK!
47

THERE SHE IS!
YES, IT'S HER!
THEN WE'RE SAVED!

OH, MISERY! SHE'S FAILED! SHE'S ALONE!

NO! WAIT! SHE SAYS SHE'S COME WITH OUR SAVIOUR!

HE'S CALLED "PETER"! AND-- WHAT!?! HE'S BEING HELD PRISONER BY THE PIRATES!

ALREADY!? THAT'S UNBELIEVABLE!

WORSE! THEIR CAPTAIN WANTS TO MAKE HIM ONE OF THEM!
OR ELSE USE HIM AS BAIT!!

? AS BAIT?!
YES! SOMETHING TERRIBLE IS GOING ON!
THE CAPTAIN HAS FOUND A WAY TO STEAL OUR TREASURE!
THAT'S IMPOSSIBLE! THE WATCHMAN WATCHES OVER IT!

WHAT!?
NOT FOR LONG!
THEN WE'RE DONE FOR!
END
FIRST EPISODE
48

# TUNDRA
PUBLISHING LTD.

| | |
|---|---|
| **Kevin Eastman** | ***President & Publisher*** |
| Kelly Meeks | *Vice President* |
| Mark Martin | *Art Director* |
| Paul Jenkins | *Production Director* |
| Susan Alston | *Administrative Director* |
| John Paresky | *Controller* |
| Marie Lisewski | *Executive Assistant to the Publisher/ Contract Manager* |
| Greg S. Baisden | *Managing Editor* |
| Ann Eagan | *Director of Promotions* |
| Tamara Sibert | *Advertising Art Director* |
| Steven Ohlson-Wardlaw | *Distribution Manager* |
| Kevin Russell | *Marketing Manager* |
| Marc Arsenault, Michael Eastman, Deb McConnell | *Production Assistants* |
| John Wills | *Warehouse Manager* |
| Victor Lisewski | *Warehouse crew* |
| Philip Amara | *Production Coordinator* |
| Jeannie Martin, Denise McKenna, Sherri Sullivan | *Accounting* |
| Beth Robinson | *Receptionist* |